Strawberries are sweet!
They sometimes look like
the shape of a human heart!

This book is given with love...

To:

_____

From:

_____

When You Have

LOVE

WRITTEN BY KIRA SIENES CORONA

ILLUSTRATED BY GLORIA E. RATAR

When you have love
You have a special gift,
To give to someone
Whose heart needs a lift.

Love can be given,

In more than one way,

To make a big difference
In somebody's day.

Love can be felt
Through a warm embrace...

And can help a friend
Feel accepted and safe.

Love can be found
Waiting in line,

When learning to be patient
Until the right time.

Love can be hard,
A hard thing to do!

And sometimes you won't
Want to say, "I love you."

Love can be heard
When forgiving your sister,

Your parents, your brother,
Or even a stranger.

Love can be selfless,
Letting others go first...

It gives time and is kind
To those at their worst.

Love can be gracious
When you make mistakes,

Leaving room to grow,
Passing all the heartaches.

And love can be strong!

That's the best part you see...

It can carry the world,

Carry you,
Carry me.

Love knows no differences,

It just sees you for you...

And when you have love,
It can carry you through.

"But the fruit of the Spirit is LOVE, joy, peace, patience, kindness, goodness, faithfulness, gentleness, self-control; against such things there is no law."

GALATIANS 5:22-23 ESV

Write the names of the people in your
life who fill your heart with love!

🐾 Claim Your FREE Gift!

Visit ➡  <u>PDICBooks.com/Gift</u>

Thank you for purchasing "When You Have Love," and welcome to the Puppy Dogs & Ice Cream family.

We're certain you're going to love the little gift we've prepared for you at the website above.

CPSIA information can be obtained
at www.ICGtesting.com
Printed in the USA
LVHW071411080222
710589LV00015B/978

9 781953 177865